H469m

THE MIDNIGHT EATERS

AMY HEST

Illustrated by

KAREN GUNDERSHEIMER

Four Winds Press   New York

Four Winds Press, Macmillan Publishing Company,
866 Third Avenue, New York, NY 10022. Collier Macmillan Canada, Inc.
Printed and bound in Singapore.   First American Edition.   10   9   8   7   6   5   4   3   2   1

The text of this book is set in 16 point Icone 45 Light.
The illustrations are rendered in pencil and gouache on white and colored paper, and are reproduced in full color.

Two of the turn-of-the-century photographs in Nana's album were inspired by images in *Jessie Tarbox Beals:
First Woman's News Photographer* by Alexander Alland, Sr. I gratefully acknowledge my debt to that work
and to Sandra Berler, who brought it to my attention.—KG

Library of Congress Cataloging-in-Publication Data
Hest, Amy. The midnight eaters/by Amy Hest; illustrated by Karen Gundersheimer.   p.   cm.
Summary: Despite the doctor's warning that she is too frail, Samantha's grandmother zestfully joins her in a
midnight raid on the kitchen, where they make fabulous ice-cream sundaes and look at old photographs.
ISBN 0-02-743630-6
[1. Grandmothers—Fiction. 2. Old age—Fiction.] I. Gundersheimer, Karen, ill. II. Title.
PZ7.H4375Mi 1989   [E]—dc19   88-24381 CIP AC

For my grandmother,
who was a splendid roommate.
—A.H.

With much love to
John, Ann, Adam, and Jake.
—K.G.

It's midnight now, and everyone is sleeping.

Except Samantha J. Blustein. Here she is, wide awake and tucked in tight, twisting right and flipping left.

She leans on two elbows to check on her grandmother in the bunk below. "Nana," she whispers, "are you up?"

"You bet I am." Nana lifts an arm toward the slender angle of moonlight. The round gold watch that used to be on Grampa's wrist is way too big for her freckled one; yet she wears it every single day, and every night, too.

Sam flops back. She fluffs the pillow, then punches it flat. And she works on her balancing act, slowly stretching toes to the ceiling as Bear wobbles in the curves of her feet. "How come you're not sleeping?" she says.

"Because," answers Nana, "this old house of yours is twitching like crazy."

"Are you scared? It's only wind." Sam does not feel as brave as she sounds. That wind's a wild one tonight, making unseen circles out there and scooping her name from the air.... Samantha J. Blustein ... come and play....

"My city apartment doesn't twitch," brags Nana, "and it never groans and creaks."

"Why not?" says Sam.

"Well, it's home, I guess."

Samantha thinks about that. Then she says, "Are you sad to be my roommate now? It's only for a while, you know, until the doctor says you're better."

"Sad?" Nana sounds surprised. "You are a splendid roommate, Samantha J., the very best around."

Sam smiles in the dark.

"It's a good thing," says Nana in her making-mischief voice, "a very good thing, you aren't hungry."

"But I am!" Sam wails. "*Painfully* hungry." Skipping the ladder, she leaps toward the braided rug, silent as a parachutist and just as grand. "I will bring us a snack," she announces, groping for slippers and the socks she left somewhere.

"Nonsense."

"But I can be quiet," promises Sam, "and no one else will know."

"Nonsense." Nana says it again, then reaches for her glasses, the pretty ones that slide down her nose when she reads. "I am going with you."

"You're supposed to stay *put,*" scolds Sam. "Doctor's orders. Lots of rest."

"Well, phooey to the doctor. Ile's just a kid."

"What about my mother, Nana?"

"Not a word to *her*! Now, get your robe, there on the rocker." And she turns on both heels, taking soft-as-feather steps toward the bedroom door.

Nana goes first. Past the parents' room, like a pair
of thieves in the night.

Down the stairs.
They stretch across
number seven, the squeaker.

"Scared?" whispers Nana.

"Not a bit," Sam lies.

"Well, good."

Nana gives the swinging kitchen door a push and quickly flicks the row of lights.

Sam takes stock. "Apples!"
she calls. "Oranges and
pears, bread and jelly,
leftover chicken, and celery
sticks."

   "Are you forgetting the
freezer, Sam?"

"Ah-ha! It's ice cream
you're after!" She pulls over
the step stool. "I see
chocolate, vanilla...and,
way in back, my mother's
fancy butter pecan."

   "Not a bad start."

"Here's the scooper, Nana."

"Now, two bowls. Preferably large."

Sam kicks off furry slippers and climbs across counters to reach her favorite lime green ones.

"You can't make a proper ice cream sundae without whipped cream. And," adds Nana, "don't forget the chocolate syrup!"

So here they are. Sam rolls her tongue over and under the silvery spoon. She makes happy little noises like *mmmnnn* and *aaammm*. She smacks her lips and seals her lashes to hold the taste a smidgen more. Nana smacks her lips, too.

"I wish Grampa were here with us now."

Nana doesn't answer, but Sam can tell she's wishing it, too.

"It isn't fair, you know, that Grampa had to die."

"Well, it *isn't* fair." Nana sighs. "It's just the way things are, I guess."

"Will you die, too?"

"Of course I will! But I'm not ready yet." Nana winks. Her eyes are palest blue.

"But what does the doctor say?"

"Ach, the doctor!" Nana waves a fist in the air. "A nice enough boy, but he worries too much!"

"He thinks you are frail. I heard him say so, to my mother."

"Frail! Schmail!" Nana sings. "Let me remind you, frail old ladies do *not* eat ice-cream sundaes on snowy winter nights." She lowers her voice to a whisper. "And don't tell your mother."

"Promise."

Suddenly Nana skitters clear across the room. She bends carefully, holding one hand across the back of her waist, to pull something from the corner cupboard.

"Is it old picture time?" asks Sam, knowing that it is.

The familiar scrapbook is boldest red and thick with memories, and the pages inside have ragged edges trimmed in gold. Nana turns them one by one.

"Who's the girl?" Sam teases.

"Why, that's me!"

"*You?*" Sam pretends to be surprised. "But, Nana, *you* are old."

"I wasn't always."

Sam leans toward the girl in the picture. She's seen her a dozen times at least, and still she can't figure this one for Nana—this bright-eyed girl in the funny, old-fashioned dress and beads.

"Were you happy then?"

"I was young and pretty." Nana smiles. "And popular, too."

"Is it awful being old?"

"Not awful. But different."

Sam frowns. "Different how?"

"Everyone wants to take care of me!" Nana complains.

"I know," says Sam. "*You* like taking care of everyone else."

Nana examines a tall man in spectacles. He wears a pin-striped suit and smokes the fattest cigar imaginable. "Your grampa!" she announces, very proud.

"It's no wonder you married *him*. Mr. Handsome."

"He loved me," Nana whispers.

"Well, so do I." Sam snuggles close. "I have an idea," she says between two big yawns. "It's about another meeting, late at night. We can look at pictures in the album, Nana."

"And have splendid ice-cream sundaes!"

"We'll call ourselves the midnight eaters, and no one else will know. And you can take care of *me*," Sam says, "just like always."

"Now there's a fine idea." And from the way Nana says it, Sam suspects there will be another meeting of the midnight eaters. She hopes it's sometime soon.

Maybe even tomorrow.